Nate The Great
and The
Pillowcase

Nate the Great
and The
Pillowcase

by Marjorie Weinman Sharmat
and Rosalind Weinman

illustrations by Marc Simont

A Yearling Book

Text copyright © 1993 by Marjorie Weinman Sharmat and Rosalind Weinman
Illustrations copyright © 1993 by Marc Simont
Extra Fun Activities copyright © 2006 by Emily Costello
Extra Fun Activities illustrations copyright © 2006 by Laura Hart

Visit us on the Web! www.randomhouse.com/kids

**Educators and librarians, for a variety of teaching tools,
visit us at www.randomhouse.com/teachers**

ISBN: 0-440-41015-0

Reprinted by arrangement with Delacorte Press
Printed in the United States of America
One Previous Edition
May 2006
38 37 36 35 34 33 32

For our wonderful mother and father,
Anna and Nathan Weinman

With love,
M.W.S. and R.W.

I, Nate the Great, am a sleepy detective.

My dog, Sludge, is a sleepy dog.

We have just finished a sleepy case.

It started a few hours ago.

It was two o'clock in the morning.

I was not busy.

I was sleeping.

Sludge was sleeping.

Suddenly the telephone rang.

It woke us up.

Who could be calling me

in the middle of the night?

"Hello," I yawned.

It was Rosamond.

"A pillowcase is missing," she said.

"Can you help me find it?"

"No," I said, and I hung up.

The telephone rang again.

I answered it.

"Sleep on another pillowcase,"
I said.

"It's not my pillowcase,"
Rosamond said.

"It belongs to Big Hex."

"Your cat has a pillowcase?"

"Of course," Rosamond said.

I yawned. "You want me to get up
from my sleep to look for
a cat's pillowcase?"

"Yes. I thought that
Big Hex could sleep without it.
But he keeps pacing
up and down,
up and down,
up and down. . . ."
"Doesn't he have a pillow to sleep on?"
"Of course. That's why he
needs the pillowcase."
Rosamond was strange in the daytime.
But she was even more strange
at night. I knew that she
would not let me sleep.
"I will take your pillowcase case,"
I said.
I put on my bathrobe and slippers.
I wrote a note to my mother.

Dear Mother,
I know you are asleep.
I wish I were.
I am looking for a pillowcase
instead of sleeping on one.
I will be back.
Love, Nate The Great

Sludge and I went out into the night.
It was damp, dark, dreary, and shivery.
We hurried to Rosamond's house.
Rosamond looked sleepy and strange,
but not in that order.
Her four cats were there.
Plain Hex, Little Hex, and
Super Hex were asleep.

11

Big Hex was pacing up and down.
I said, "What does his pillowcase
look like?"
"It's beautiful," Rosamond said.
"I made it myself.
I made four of them.
One for each cat.
All the same.
White with holes around the
open end, and a pretty ribbon
through the holes. See?"
Rosamond pointed to her
sleeping cats.
"Big Hex's pillowcase looks
exactly like theirs?" I asked.
"Oh, no. Big Hex likes to
play with his case.

So now it's slashed and shredded.
I keep washing it.
So it's also shrunken and shriveled.
And he chewed up the ribbon.
So that's gone."
"Let me get this straight.
The missing pillowcase is
slashed and shredded,
shrunken and shriveled.
And it has holes around one end.
And you want it *back*?"
Rosamond smiled.

"Yes, Big Hex just loves it."

"When was the last time you saw it?"

"This afternoon.

I washed all my cats' things.

I had four laundry bags full.

One for each cat.

I even washed the bags.

Then I hung everything out to dry."

"Did you hang four pillowcases?"

"Of course," Rosamond said.

"One for each cat.

Then Annie came over with Fang.

I told her this was

my big laundry day for pets.

So we undressed Fang,

and I washed his sweater

and neck bandanna.
Then I hung them out to dry."
"Then what?"
"When everything was dry,
I put it all in my laundry basket."
"Were the four pillowcases there?"
"Yes."
"Then what?"
"I brought the basket into the house

and dumped everything on my bed.
Then Annie and I tried
to dress Fang in his nice clean clothes.
Well, that's the last time I'll ever try
to dress that dog!"

"What happened?"

"Fang growled at me. He showed every
one of his teeth. I ran out of the room.
Then I yelled to Annie
to take Fang's clothes home,
and to take Fang with them.
And that's what she did."

"Did you go back to your laundry
after that?"

"No. My cats were hungry,
so I fed them.
Then I read to my cats."

"You read to your cats?"
"Fifteen minutes each day."
"When did you get back to
your laundry?"
"Just before I went to bed.
I looked for the night things.

The pillowcases and nightshirts.
That's when I found out
that Big Hex's pillowcase was missing.
And one of Little Hex's nightshirts."

"You are missing the pillowcase *and*
a nightshirt?"

"No. I know where the nightshirt is.
Annie took it by mistake. I think she
just grabbed stuff in her arms
when she left."

"Aha! Perhaps Annie took Big Hex's
pillowcase by mistake."

"No," Rosamond said. "I called her
before I called you."

"You woke her, too?"

"Well, I found out that she has

Little Hex's nightshirt.
But she doesn't have the pillowcase.
See what a good detective I am?"
I, Nate the Great, yawned.
"Since you are such a good detective,
solve this case," I said.
"Sludge and I are going back to sleep."

"Wait," Rosamond said.
"I'm not a *great* detective.
You solve this case."
"Perhaps your pillowcase is
still in this room,
or you lost it
between the clothesline
and this room.
Sludge and I will look."
Sludge and I looked inside.
And outside. No luck.

I said, "Tell me,
has anyone else been in this room?"
"Only Annie and Fang and my cats."
"Very well. I must go to
Annie's house.
Call her and tell her
I'm coming."
Sludge and I went out into the night.
It was colder than before.
I wrapped my bathrobe tighter around me.
I flashed my flashlight on the ground.

Perhaps Annie had taken the
pillowcase and did not know it.
Perhaps she had dropped it
between Rosamond's house
and her own house.
But I did not see it.
Annie was waiting inside her house.
Fang was waiting, too. He was wearing
pajamas and a nightcap.
Fang had more clothes than I did.
Fang yawned. His teeth had never
looked bigger.
Annie said, "I know why you're here.
But I don't have the pillowcase.
Here is what happened.
Fang and I went over
to Rosamond's house.

Fang was wearing his neck bandanna
and the sweater I got him
for his birthday.
Fang looked very snazzy.
But after Rosamond washed
and dried his clothes,

Fang didn't want to wear them.
He growled at Rosamond.
She ran out of the room.
I stuffed Fang's clothes
into a laundry bag,
and we left fast."
"Aha," I said. "You were in a hurry."
"Yes. I even took Little Hex's
nightshirt by mistake.
I found it when Rosamond
called me up.
I looked in Rosamond's laundry bag.
I saw Fang's sweater and bandanna
and Little Hex's nightshirt.
Tomorrow I'm going to give back
the nightshirt and the laundry bag."
"Could you also have grabbed

Big Hex's pillowcase by mistake?"
Annie shrugged. "I don't know.
But it's not in the laundry bag now."
"Did you stop anywhere
on the way home?"
"Yes, at Uncle Ned's Day and Night Diner
to get some bones for Fang.

They save him some of their leftovers."
"Aha! Something could have dropped
out of the laundry bag
at the diner,
or between Rosamond's house
and the diner,
or between the diner
and your house.
What streets did you take
to and from the diner?"
"I went the shortest way.
Fang led me.
All the dogs know the shortest way."

Sludge wagged his tail.
He liked the diner.
I thanked Annie for her help.
Then Sludge and I walked out
into the night.
It seemed colder and darker.
"To the diner," I said to Sludge.

Sludge led the way.

I flashed my flashlight.

I did not see the pillowcase.

Sludge and I went inside.

The man behind the counter

looked down at Sludge.

He said, "Every dog in town

must have been in here today.

But lucky you,

I have a big bone left."

Sludge was a happy dog.

I saw pancakes on the menu.

I was an unhappy detective.

I had no money.

But I spoke up.

"I am Nate the Great.

Ned knows me.

I would like five pancakes
and some clues.
I will pay you tomorrow.
Right now I am looking
for a cat's pillowcase."
The man smiled and turned away.
He started to make the pancakes.

I saw a white cloth sticking
out of his back pocket.
Hmmm.
I peered over the counter
to take a closer look.
But the man grabbed the cloth
and wiped the counter with it.
The cloth was small and shredded, and
it had plenty of holes.
Was this the pillowcase?

Was the case solved?
The man put a plate of pancakes
in front of me.
I ate and thought.
Annie must have taken the pillowcase
by mistake and stuffed it
into the laundry bag.
When she stopped at the diner,
the pillowcase fell out.
After Annie and Fang left,

the man saw the pillowcase
and thought it was a rag.
I, Nate the Great, had to be sure.
I had to get that rag!
The man stuffed it back
into his pocket.
Then he bent over.
So did I, Nate the Great.
I reached for the rag.

I pulled it out of his pocket.
I spread it out.
I tried to open it up.
It wouldn't open.
It was not a pillowcase.
It was just a rag.
I stuffed it back
into the man's pocket.
It was time to leave.
But Sludge had not finished
his bone.
"Do you have a doggie bag?" I asked.
The man handed me a bag.
I put the bone
in the bag.
"You can finish your bone at home,"
I said to Sludge.

Sludge and I went out into the night.
"Now we must walk the streets
between the diner and
Rosamond's house,"
I said. "Lead the way."
Sludge and I walked and walked.
I did not see the pillowcase.
I saw newspapers being delivered.
I heard the clinking of milk bottles.
I saw the sun coming up.
"The moon is going down
and the sun is coming up,
and I still have not
solved this case," I said.
Sludge was sniffing the doggie bag.
Suddenly he put his teeth into it.

CRUNCH!!!
He ripped the bag and grabbed the bone.
Was Sludge hungry,
or was he trying to tell me something?
Where was the pillowcase?
We could not find it
at Rosamond's house.
It was not in the laundry bag
that Annie took home.

We could not find it
on the streets
or in the diner.
Perhaps there was something
Rosamond and Annie had not told me.
But they had told me
the same story about
what had happened
at Rosamond's house.
Except . . . for one small thing!
Suddenly I knew that
Rosamond and Annie
had both been wrong.
"Come!" I said to Sludge.
Sludge and I rushed back
to Annie's house.

It was hard to do.
My bed slippers were wearing out.
Annie was still awake.
I was glad about that.
Fang was fast asleep.
I was glad about that, too.
"I, Nate the Great, know
where the pillowcase is," I said.

"*You* have it."

"No, I don't," Annie said.

"It is not in the laundry bag."

"I, Nate the Great, say
that is because
it *is* the laundry bag!
You were in a hurry
when you left Rosamond's house.

You grabbed what you thought
was a laundry bag."
"Well, it looked like one,"
Annie said. "It was open
on one end, and it
had holes around the end.
Except the rope was missing
from the holes."

39

"The holes were for a ribbon,"
I said. "But that does not matter.
Please show it to me."
Annie ran out of the room.
She came back holding up
something white, slashed,
shredded, shrunken, and shriveled.
And full of holes at one end.
"That is Big Hex's pillowcase," I said.
"I was so busy thinking about
the things you carried from
Rosamond's house
that I did not think about
what you carried them *in.*
When Sludge went after his bone
inside a bag tonight,

he only cared about the bone,
not what the bone was in.
Sludge and I were thinking alike."
Sludge wagged his tail.
"We were thinking wrong."
Sludge slunk.
"But how did you *know* that
the laundry bag
wasn't really a laundry bag?"
Annie asked.

I, Nate the Great, smiled.
"Rosamond thought you took
the laundry in your arms.
But you told me that you took it
in a laundry bag.
So why wasn't Rosamond
missing a laundry bag?
Because you never took one!"
Annie was staring at the pillowcase.

"Big Hex sleeps on *this?*" she said.
"It's ugly."
Annie tossed the pillowcase to me.
"My Fang would never
sleep on anything so ugly."
Fang heard his name.
He woke up.
He sniffed the ripped doggie bag.
"Pleasant dreams," I said.

Sludge and I walked to
Rosamond's house.
Slowly.
I now had holes
on the bottoms
of both slippers.
"This case is over," I said
to Sludge. "Now Big Hex can
go to sleep.
You can go to sleep.
I can go to sleep."
I rang Rosamond's doorbell.
I waited.
I rang it again.
I waited.
At last the door opened.
Rosamond was standing there.

Yawning.

"You woke me up!" she said.

"I, Nate the Great, have
solved your case."

I held up the pillowcase.
"Annie took this by mistake.
She thought it was a laundry bag."
Rosamond grabbed the pillowcase.
"Thanks. Big Hex will
get a good night's sleep
tomorrow night."
"What about now?"
"Oh, he got tired of pacing.
He's been sleeping since
you left the house.
Nighty night, Nate."
Rosamond slammed the door.
I, Nate the Great, was mad.
But I was glad that
the case was over.

Sludge and I went home.
We went to bed.
It felt good.
The telephone rang.
I, Nate the Great, answered it.
I knew exactly what to say.
"Wrong number."

~ Extra ~
Fun Activities!

What's Inside

Super Hex sleeps on a pillowcase that has seen better days. Nate found out about some more animals with strange sleep habits.

NATE'S NOTES:
Funny Ways Animals Sleep

Dolphins sleep with one eye open! That allows one side of their brain to rest while the other side stays wide awake!

Turtles sleep buried in muck! In the winter, pond turtles burrow into the mud to hibernate. The cold weather slows their bodies down. They get all the oxygen they need through their skin. They sleep until spring.

Bats sleep upside down! Their feet cling to a twig or board. In the cold, they huddle together for warmth. That works really well — because their colonies can be huge! Some Mexican free-tail bat colonies have 20 million members.

Horses sometimes sleep standing up! Their back legs lock into position so that standing is almost as comfy as lying down.

Flamingos often sleep standing on one leg! During storms, they face into the wind to stop rain from soaking their feathers. Sometimes the blowing wind will make them sway. Rock-a-bye, baby. . . .

Some sharks sleep while swimming! They need the movement of water over their gills to take in oxygen, so they are always on the move. Other species stop moving and push water over their gills with their fins.

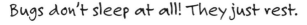

Bugs don't sleep at all! They just rest.

NATE'S NOTES:
People Who Work at Night

Sometimes sleepy detectives crack cases at night. They're not alone. About 20 million Americans work the graveyard shift. Here are some of the people working while you dream:

DOCTORS AND NURSES staff emergency rooms 24 hours a day. They also watch over patients in the hospital.

NEWS REPORTERS gather information all night long. It's always daytime somewhere on the planet. They send out stories in newspapers, on the radio and TV, and on the Internet.

TRUCK DRIVERS move food and other products across the country all night.

POLICE OFFICERS patrol dark streets and highways.

MAIL CARRIERS sort packages. They load them onto trucks and planes. The packages are ready to be delivered in the morning.

FIREFIGHTERS are ready to hop into action even in the wee hours.

COOKS AND SERVERS work at some restaurants and shops 24/7. Night workers need to eat too!

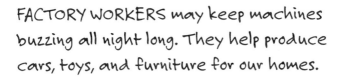

FACTORY WORKERS may keep machines buzzing all night long. They help produce cars, toys, and furniture for our homes.

BAKERS make bread, cakes, and cookies in the middle of the night—so kids can eat them in the morning!

ASTRONOMERS gaze at the night sky, learning about planets and stars far away.

CLEANERS scrub office buildings late at night so that they sparkle for daytime workers.

PARENTS soothe children who have bad dreams—even when it's much too late for little people to be awake.

12

How to Make a Diner Recipe: Grilled Cheese Sandwich

Diners are often open late at night. They serve "comfort food." That might mean pancakes for one person and grilled cheese for another. This sandwich tastes good during the day, too.

Ask an adult to help you with this recipe.

GET TOGETHER:

- 2 slices of bread
- 2 slices of cheese. American melts well, but you can use whatever kind you like.
- 2 slices of tomato (if you like)
- a frying pan
- 1 pat of butter, cut in half
- a spatula

MAKE YOUR GRILLED CHEESE:

1. Assemble your sandwich: Place both slices of cheese between the slices of bread. Slip in the tomato, too, if you're using some.
2. Place the frying pan over medium heat.
3. Add half of the butter to the pan. Allow the butter to melt.
4. Put the sandwich in the pan. Cook for about three minutes. Scoot it around so that the bread soaks up all the melted butter.

5. Flip the sandwich. Add the rest of the butter to the pan. Scoot the sandwich around again.
6. Cook until the cheese is oozy.
7. Watch carefully to make sure the sandwich isn't getting too brown. If it is, turn down the heat.
8. Remove the sandwich from the pan. Serve diner style—with a pickle! Eat!

Funny Pages

Q: Why did the kid put sugar under his pillow?
A: He wanted sweet dreams!

Q: Why do you go to bed?
A: Because the bed won't come to you!

Q: What happened to the lady who dreamed she was eating a cloud?
A: She woke up and her pillow was gone!

Q: What kind of bed does a mermaid sleep in?
A: A waterbed!

Q: What has a bed but doesn't sleep?
A: A river!

Q: Why did the boy take a pencil to bed?
A: To draw the curtains!

Q: What did the blanket say to the bed?
A: I've got you covered!

Q: Why did the girl take a ruler to bed?
A: She wanted to see how long she slept.

Q: Why shouldn't you believe a person who's in bed?
A: Because he's lying.

Q: What did the detective say from beneath the sheets?
A: Shhh! I'm under cover.

Q: Why did the detective put on skates before going to bed?
A: Because he wanted to get rolling first thing in the morning.

Q: What do you call a mummy eating cookies in bed?
A: A crummy mummy!

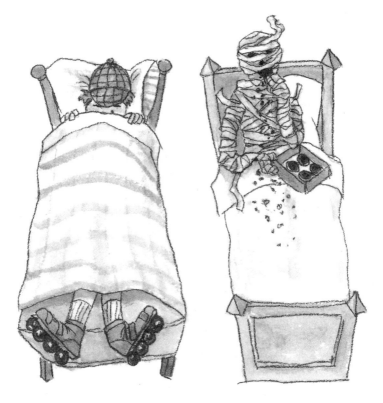

How to Make a Bedtime Snack: Oatmeal Cookies

Some foods help you sleep. Try eating oatmeal cookies with milk. You'll soon be dozing!

Ask an adult to help you with this recipe.

GET TOGETHER:

- ³/₄ cup of brown sugar, firmly packed
- ¹/₂ cup of white sugar
- 1 stick of butter
- 2 mixing bowls
- an electric mixer
- 1 egg
- 1 teaspoon of vanilla
- 1¹/₂ cups of flour

- 1 teaspoon of baking soda
- 1 teaspoon of salt
- 1 teaspoon of cinnamon
- 3 cups of oats (quick or old-fashioned)
- a wooden spoon
- $\frac{1}{2}$ cup of raisins
- a cookie sheet
- a wire rack

MAKE YOUR COOKIES:

1. Preheat the oven to 375 °F.
2. Add both sugars and the butter to one of the bowls. Using the electric mixer, beat together until fluffy.
3. Beat in the egg and the vanilla.

4. Combine the flour, baking soda, salt, and cinnamon in the other bowl.
5. Add the dry ingredients to the wet ones. Mix well.
6. Add the oats. Stir them into the batter with the wooden spoon.
7. Add the raisins. Mix them in.

8. Scoop up a tablespoon of batter. Place it on the cookie sheet. Fill the sheet with about 12 cookies, evenly spaced.
9. Bake for 8 minutes.
10. Remove the cookies from the oven and let them cool slightly on the cookie sheet before moving them to the wire rack.
11. Serve with a glass of milk just before bedtime. Sweet dreams!

More Snoozy Snacks

Up late? These snacks contain elements that make you feel dozy. Eating them will help you fall asleep.

Apple pie and ice cream

Cereal with milk and banana slices

A peanut butter sandwich

Cottage cheese and crackers

Scrambled eggs and toast

A whole-wheat pita and hummus

A tuna salad sandwich

How to Make Fuzzy Slippers

Nate needs new slippers. How about you?

GET TOGETHER:

- 1 piece of fake fur (it should be as big as both flip-flops laid side by side)*
- 1 pair of flip-flops
- 1 marking pen
- fabric scissors
- double-sided tape (carpet tape is best, if you can find it)

*You can buy this at a craft store.

MAKE YOUR SLIPPERS

1. Place the fabric on a flat surface, fur side down.
2. Put one flip-flop on the fabric. Trace around it with the marker. Repeat with the other flip-flop.
3. Cut out the shapes.
4. On each cutout, mark the three places where the foot straps join the bottom of the shoe.

5. Carefully cut a slit from the edge of the cutout to each mark.
6. Cover the top of each flip-flop with double-sided tape.
7. Starting at the heel, roll the cutout over the tape, fur side up. Fit the slits around the foot straps. Push the fabric down so that it sticks to the tape.
8. Wear your slippers on your nighttime adventures!

Have you helped solve all
Nate the Great's mysteries?

❏ **Nate the Great**: Meet Nate, the great detective, and join him as he uses incredible sleuthing skills to solve his first big case.

❏ **Nate the Great Goes Undercover**: Who— or what—is raiding Oliver's trash every night? Nate bravely hides out in his friend's garbage can to catch the smelly crook.

❏ **Nate the Great and the Lost List**: Nate loves pancakes, but who ever heard of cats eating them? Is a strange recipe at the heart of this mystery?

❏ **Nate the Great and the Phony Clue**: Against ferocious cats, hostile adversaries, and a sly phony clue, Nate struggles to prove that he's still the world's greatest detective.

❏ **Nate the Great and the Sticky Case**: Nate is stuck with his stickiest case yet as he hunts for his friend Claude's valuable stegosaurus stamp.

❏ **Nate the Great and the Missing Key**: Nate isn't afraid to look anywhere—even under the nose of his friend's ferocious dog, Fang—to solve the case of the missing key.

❑ **Nate the Great and the Snowy Trail**: Nate has his work cut out for him when his friend Rosamond loses the birthday present she was going to give him. How can he find the present when Rosamond won't even tell him what it is?

❑ **Nate the Great and the Fishy Prize**: The trophy for the Smartest Pet Contest has disappeared! Will Sludge, Nate's clue-sniffing dog, help solve the case and prove he's worthy of the prize?

❑ **Nate the Great Stalks Stupidweed**: When his friend Oliver loses his special plant, Nate searches high and low. Who knew a little weed could be so tricky?

❑ **Nate the Great and the Boring Beach Bag**: It's no relaxing day at the beach for Nate and his trusty dog, Sludge, as they search through sand and surf for signs of a missing beach bag.

❑ **Nate the Great Goes Down in the Dumps**: Nate discovers that the only way to clean up this case is to visit the town dump. Detective work can sure get dirty!

❑ **Nate the Great and the Halloween Hunt**: It's Halloween, but Nate isn't trick-or-treating for candy. Can any of the witches, pirates, and robots he meets help him find a missing cat?

❑ **Nate the Great and the Musical Note**: Nate is used to looking for clues, not listening for them! When he gets caught in the middle of a musical riddle, can he hear his way out?

- **Nate the Great and the Stolen Base**: It's not easy to track down a stolen base, and Nate's hunt leads him to some strange places before he finds himself at bat once more.

- **Nate the Great and the Pillowcase**: When a pillowcase goes missing, Nate must venture into the dead of night to search for clues. Everyone sleeps easier knowing Nate the Great is on the case!

- **Nate the Great and the Mushy Valentine**: Nate hates mushy stuff. But when someone leaves a big heart taped to Sludge's doghouse, Nate must help his favorite pooch discover his secret admirer.

- **Nate the Great and the Tardy Tortoise**: Where did the mysterious green tortoise in Nate's yard come from? Nate needs all his patience to follow this slow . . . slow . . . clue.

- **Nate the Great and the Crunchy Christmas**: It's Christmas, and Fang, Annie's scary dog, is not feeling jolly. Can Nate find Fang's crunchy Christmas mail before Fang crunches on *him*?

- **Nate the Great Saves the King of Sweden**: Can Nate solve his *first-ever* international case without leaving his own neighborhood?

- **Nate the Great and Me: The Case of the Fleeing Fang**: A surprise Happy Detective Day party is great fun for Nate until his friend's dog disappears! Help Nate track down the missing pooch, and learn all the tricks of the trade in a special fun section for aspiring detectives.